frog goes to dinner

by mercer mayer

dial books for young readers
new york

For Tereska and Bob

Published by Dial Books for Young Readers
A division of Penguin Young Readers Group
345 Hudson Street
New York, New York 10014

ISBN 0-8037-2884-0
Library of Congress Catalog Card Number: 74-2881
Manufactured in China on acid-free paper

1 3 5 7 9 10 8 6 4 2

RAMS
MY Box
KEEP OUT

FANCY
RESTAURANT

MENU

FIRE
EXIT

FIRE
EXIT

FIRE
EXIT